STICK DOG

TAKES OUT SUSHI

STICK DOG

TAKES OUT SUSHI

By Tom Watson

HARPER

An Imprint of HarperCollinsPublishers

Library of Congress Control Number: 2020946931

ISBN 978-0-06-301427-5

20 21 22 23 24 PC/LSCH 10 9 8 7 6 5 4 3 2 1

❖

First Edition

Dedicated to MEJ

(LOFCTLY)

TABLE OF CONTENTS

Chapter 1

RUMBLE

Mutt, Poo-Poo, and Stripes were all asleep in Stick Dog's pipe.

Rumble.

That was Mutt. Well, it was Mutt's stomach.

When Mutt's belly rumbled, it *really* rumbled. He was the biggest—and shaggiest—dog in the gang. And when his stomach rumbled inside

Stick Dog's pipe, that sound echoed for several seconds before fading to silence.

Karen noticed the noise—and scrunched up her face.

The sound must have disturbed Mutt too. He shifted position slightly as he slept, rolling over from his left side to his right in an unconscious attempt to quiet his belly.

It didn't work.

Rumble.

"Stick Dog," Karen said quietly. "Is there anything you can do about this? I'm super-tired and need to take a nap."

Stick Dog looked at all his friends. Poo-Poo

and Stripes were asleep, resting comfortably side by side. Mutt shifted his body again. Only Karen was awake—and bothered.

"I don't think there's anything I can do," Stick Dog said. It had been a long afternoon. They had spent most of the day looking for food—without finding much of anything. Their only success came at Picasso Park where Poo-Poo had found a couple of stale hamburger buns beneath a picnic table. They had shared those. "Everybody's stomach rumbles at some point. Mutt's just hungry."

Rumble.

"I know," Karen said, understanding. "I'm hungry too."

Stick Dog said, "We all are."

"Why can't we just go see Lucy at the meat store?" Karen asked hopefully. "I bet she can get us something."

Stick Dog wished it could be that easy. Their new friend Lucy, a German shepherd who lived in the back room of a meat shop in town, couldn't help them today.

"Lucy went on vacation with her human roommate, remember?" Stick Dog said. "She told us a few days ago. The meat store is closed—and she's not even there."

"Oh, right," replied Karen. "I forgot."

Rumble.

"I think maybe you should take a different approach to this whole thing," Stick Dog whispered to Karen. He could tell that Karen grew a little more annoyed every time Mutt's stomach made noise.

 Karen looked up at Stick Dog and asked, "What do you mean?"

"Well, Mutt doesn't really have a choice about when his stomach rumbles," Stick Dog said quietly. "But you have a choice about how you react to it."

"How so?"

"You see, right now his rumbling stomach is bothering you and keeping you awake," Stick Dog explained. "But I think if you change your attitude a little, you'll find that sound can actually be rather pleasant and comforting."

Karen looked up skeptically at Stick Dog. She doubted his idea.

"Why don't you lie down here closer to me and I'll explain," Stick Dog said.

Rumble.

Karen shrugged her shoulders and plopped down next to Stick Dog.

"Now, close your eyes," Stick Dog said in a calm, soothing voice.

Karen closed her eyes.

"Let's pretend that sound is something totally different," he whispered. "Why don't we say that sound isn't coming from Mutt at all? Let's imagine that it's actually a rainstorm off in the distance."

Karen nodded silently.

Rumble.

"And that rumbling sound is thunder,"

Stick Dog continued. "It's not loud, violent thunder that startles you. It's a rolling, vibrating thunder that's miles and miles from here. You can hear it get softer and softer as the storm moves farther and farther away. You hear the rainfall outside. The raindrops fall from the sky and splash gently against the trees. They splatter quietly on the ground."

Karen's body relaxed as Stick Dog spoke.

Rumble.

"There's the thunder again," he whispered. "Getting farther and farther away. There's a dull gray flash of lightning. The wind swooshes slowly and peacefully through the forest. The tree branches brush and rustle against each other. It's a peaceful sound. A

calming sound. A sleepy sound."

Stick Dog looked down at Karen.

"A sleepy sound," he repeated.

She breathed slow, rhythmic breaths.

"A sleepy sound."

Rumble.

Stick Dog was pretty sure Karen was asleep now. That was good. He knew that after a disappointing food search during the day, they would need to go back out this evening to find something to eat. They all needed to rest.

He closed his own eyes.

But only for seven seconds.

After seven seconds, there was another sound.

It wasn't Mutt's rumbling stomach.

It was Karen.

She wasn't asleep.

Chapter 2

HOW ABOUT THAT?

"Stick Dog?" Karen whispered.

He smiled at her voice. He didn't open his eyes. He just said, "Yes?"

"It's me, Karen."

"Okay, umm, thanks for telling me," Stick Dog said.

"I just thought with your eyes closed and everything,

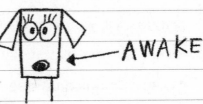

AWAKE

I should, you know, identify myself," Karen explained.

"We were just talking a few seconds ago," Stick Dog said. He did enjoy his conversations with Karen quite a lot. They could be very, well, interesting. "And neither one of us has moved."

"I just wanted you to be sure," Karen said. "You know, that it's me and my voice and everything."

"I appreciate that," Stick Dog said, trying to suppress the smile creeping onto his face as their talk continued. "But we've been friends for years now, Karen. We see each other almost every day. I recognized your voice. It's quite unique—just like you."

"What a nice thing to say, Stick Dog," Karen said with pride. "Can I ask you a question?"

"Of course."

"Could you open your eyes now?"

"Sure," Stick Dog said, and opened his eyes.

"See, Stick Dog!" Karen exclaimed, and pushed herself up. "It *is* me!"

"It sure is," he said. "How about that? It's good to see you, Karen."

"Good to see you too, Stick Dog," she replied. "I didn't take a nap after all."

"I see that," Stick Dog said. "What happened?"

"Well, I did what you said," Karen explained, and began to pace back and forth in front of Stick Dog. "I imagined that Mutt's rumbling stomach was a rainstorm and everything. And it was real peaceful and calm and all that. And, you know, the rainfall made that nice soothing sound and blah, blah, blah. All that stuff."

"But it didn't help you fall asleep?"

"No, not at all," Karen said quickly. "Do you want to know why?"

"Sure. Tell me."

"It's because all that pretending and stuff made my brain keep going."

Stick Dog tilted his head a bit to the left. He said, "I'm not quite sure what you mean."

"It's just that I couldn't *stop* pretending," Karen explained further. "So, I imagined the wind whooshing through the trees and then I thought some of the old branches and stuff would probably fall down. And I thought just how many branches would fall down in a whole forest. I mean, it could be millions and millions."

"Umm, it would be a lot, I guess. For sure."

"So, I imagined all those broken branches and sticks all over the ground in the forest,"

Karen continued. She was happy that Stick Dog was following along, you could tell. "And then I saw myself going through the forest and stepping over all those branches and sticks. And I saw Mutt there. And Poo-Poo and Stripes. You were there too, Stick Dog!"

"That's great," Stick Dog said slowly. He wasn't quite sure where all this was going. But with Karen, frankly, that was not an uncommon occurrence. "I'm glad we were all together."

"And guess what I realized as I imagined all of us out there in the forest with those million and millions of broken sticks and branches?"

"What?"

"I realized how much I really, really, really love sticks!" Karen yelped and hopped up and down a few times. "I mean, sticks are awesome. You can chew on them. You can play fetch with them. And you can carry them around and knock into stuff with them. Heck, just having a stick—you know, like totally *possessing* it—is completely and totally awesome, don't you think?"

"I, umm, like sticks too. You bet," he said.

"Well, once I imagined all those sticks, there was no way I was going to sleep," Karen said. "You know what I mean?"

"I understand," Stick Dog said, and smiled. "So, would you like to go out in the woods and find some sticks right now?"

"Yes! Yes!! Yes!!!"

But they didn't go find some sticks out in the woods right then.

No.

Mutt rolled over to face them.

"Did you guys say you want some sticks? I have some right here."

And that's when everything changed.

Chapter 3

A VERY INTERESTING TREE

Poo-Poo and Stripes woke up too.

AWAKE

"What's all this about sticks?" asked Poo-Poo after he yawned and stretched.

"I heard it too," Stripes said, and pushed herself up to standing. She shook her body to wakefulness. "What's going on?"

"It's all because of Mutt's stomach," Karen started to explain. "See, I pretended that rumbling sound was thunder during a rainstorm. Then there was a forest and wind and millions of sticks everywhere! And now I can't stop thinking about sticks!"

Poo-Poo asked, "Hunh?"

"It's a long story," Stick Dog intervened in an attempt to speed things up. "Mutt, did you say you actually have some sticks?"

"I sure do, Stick Dog," Mutt replied happily. He was always glad to provide things for his friends. "I've got plenty for everyone."

Karen, Poo-Poo, Stripes, and Stick Dog then gathered around Mutt in a circle. They all knew what would happen next.

Mutt spread his legs out a little and began
to shake. He started off slowly—just a few
little shimmies from different parts of his
body. But in just a few seconds, his few little
shimmies built into a massive, full-body,
pipe-rattling shake.

Things flew out of his fur from everywhere.
There was a pencil,
a tennis ball, two
bottle caps, a
mitten, two socks,
a water bottle, and
some other stuff.

And there were six thin wooden sticks.

"There they are," Mutt said, and stopped
shaking. The sticks had fallen pretty much
from the same place—near his right hip. "I

knew they'd come out quickly. I just found them yesterday."

Mutt gathered the other objects and placed them back into his fur. While he did that, Stick Dog, Karen, Stripes, and Poo-Poo examined the sticks.

"They're all the same size," observed Poo-Poo.

Stripes added, "And the same shape."

"They're kind of pointed on the ends," said Karen, tilting her head in curiosity. "What kind of tree would have the exact same-sized branches? I mean, that would be a pretty strange-looking tree, don't you think?"

"It would be odd," Stick Dog said. "I think maybe these sticks didn't come from a tree, Karen. Where did you find them, Mutt?"

"I ripped open a garbage bag at the end of a human's driveway last night," Mutt answered as he put the final item—the mitten—back into his fur. "The sticks were in there. I found these six loose ones. And I found two more wrapped in a paper package."

Stick Dog asked, "Do you still have that paper package?"

Mutt nodded and shook his right hip.

A skinny paper sleeve with words on it fell out of Mutt's fur. It was a little longer than the sticks and was torn open. Stick Dog went over to look at it. He read the words and he could see two sticks inside. While he did that, the others each picked up a stick with their mouths. They chewed and gnawed on them.

Karen, Poo-Poo, and Mutt all chewed on the middle of the sticks.

But Stripes did not.

She just so happened to pick up her stick from the pointy end.

She munched on that end for a few seconds. Her eyes flashed opened wide.

"That's not a regular stick!" Stripes exclaimed, dropping it from her mouth. She crouched down with her front legs, but her hips and her tail—it was wagging—were still in the air. She held the stick with both paws in front of her face, eyeballed it closely, and licked the pointy end once. Twice. Three times. "It's a flavor stick! It's got stuff on it! Look close! There are three colors—red, brown, and green! It's delicious! You have to taste the pointy end!"

This amazing information shocked the others. Mutt, Karen, and Poo-Poo all dropped their sticks immediately. They stared at them for a few seconds and then started to lick the pointy ends. Even Stick Dog hurried to lick one of the loose sticks.

In no time at all, they discovered that Stripes was correct. Those sticks did, in fact, have a distinct flavor.

"What is that?" Karen asked. "It's certainly tasty. I just don't know what it is."

But Poo-Poo did.

He always did.

Poo-Poo considered himself the leader in the group about food. He was a connoisseur, an aficionado—an expert. He sat back on his haunches and stroked a paw beneath his chin for several seconds—and then spoke.

"I'm happy to use my sophisticated and refined food-tasting abilities to explain the unique flavors on these sticks," he said. He closed his eyes halfway and swayed his head

left and right a couple
of times. He licked
his lips for a moment
before opening
his eyes fully and
addressing the group.

Karen, Mutt, and Stripes stared at him. Stick
Dog smiled a bit—and got ready to listen
too.

"You see, these are no ordinary sticks,"
he began. "They have been dipped in
flavors that are unknown to the common
and ordinary palate. But, fear not, I have
managed to discern and define their origins.
I taste three distinct layers of flavor on
this wonderful stick. The first flavor—the
red one—comes from the distant sea. It is
marine in origin."

"Fish?" Mutt asked.

"Fish," Poo-Poo confirmed, and continued. "The brown layer is familiar: it's salt. But this is no regular salt. It's been flavored and liquefied, I believe. But it is the third flavor—the green one—that brings everything together."

"What is it, Poo-Poo?" asked Mutt. "What's the third flavor?"

"I don't know the specific name," Poo-Poo admitted. "But it has enough spicy bite to awaken my taste buds in a most satisfying way. Its pasty texture has an intriguing peppery kick that binds all the flavors together into a single delicious bite."

"I have to say, Poo-Poo," Stick Dog said, "you have, once again, really nailed that description."

"But how could all these flavors be on the end of a stick?" Mutt asked, and took another lick.

Stripes asked, "And why?"

"I think I know," Karen said. She sounded pretty confident. "I think Stick Dog is probably wrong about these sticks. I think they actually *are* branches from a tree. And that tree grows all these flavors. And all these same-sized branches simply absorbed the flavors."

This theory was not questioned at all by Stripes, Mutt, or Poo-Poo.

But Stick Dog was suspicious about it.

"Karen," he said. "I'm not sure I heard you correctly. Do you believe that these flavors grow on a tree?"

"That's right."

"You think salt grows on a tree?"

"Sure."

"And spicy things—like a hot pepper or something—grows on a tree?"

"Definitely."

"And, umm, fish?" Stick Dog asked. "You think fish can grow on trees?"

"Correct-a-mundo," Karen said. "Trees are really quite magical things. They can grow anything. Apples, pears, oranges. Why, growing a few fish and some saltshakers shouldn't be any problem. I think if we want to find some more of these sticks and flavors, we just need to go into the forest and find these trees. Easy-peasy, pumpkin pie!"

"Let's look for the fish tree!" Poo-Poo exclaimed.

With that, Karen took three quick steps toward the opening of Stick Dog's pipe. Mutt, Stripes, and Poo-Poo followed right behind her.

Stick Dog did not.

"Wait! he exclaimed. He obviously had serious doubts about this whole thing. "How can a fish, umm, grow on a tree? Fish need to live in water. I'm pretty sure they can't breathe out of water."

But as he expressed his doubts, his friends seemed to be more and more convinced of the fish tree idea.

"Umm, rain, Stick Dog," Stripes answered. "Have you ever heard of it? Rain falls on the tree to help the fish."

"Wouldn't rain have to be falling constantly over the tree for the fish to grow and survive?" asked Stick Dog.

"They just hold their breath between

rainstorms," Poo-Poo explained.

Mutt added, "No big deal."

"But nobody can hold their breath that long," Stick Dog persisted politely. "It can be weeks and weeks between rainstorms. I just don't think it's possible for anybody to hold their breath that long."

"Let me demonstrate," Poo-Poo said, and stepped next to Stick Dog.

"How?"

"I'm going to hold my breath for a couple of weeks," Poo-Poo explained simply.

Stick Dog decided not to say anything else. He just waited and watched as Poo-Poo got ready to hold his breath for, umm, a couple of weeks. Mutt, Karen, and Stripes came closer to watch too.

Poo-Poo sat back on his rear legs. He closed his eyes, crossed his paws in front of his chest, and took three deep cleansing breaths. Once he reached a relaxed and meditative state, he took a great gulp of air.

And held it.

For three seconds.

His cheeks puffed out, but he kept his mouth closed.

Five seconds.

His eyes popped open wide.

Eight seconds.

His head began to wiggle and shake.

Eleven seconds.

Whooooosh!

Poo-Poo released all that air from his lungs and panted in and out quickly. He fell back to all fours once he was breathing normally.

"See?" Poo-Poo said, looking at Stick Dog directly.

"Umm, see what?" Stick Dog asked.

"See how long I held my breath, that's what," Poo-Poo responded. "How long was that?"

"I wasn't counting," Stick Dog said. He felt kind of bad that Poo-Poo would be disappointed with the results. "It seemed like about fifteen seconds or so. That's a really long time. Super-impressive."

"That proves it then," Karen said.

"Proves what?"

She answered, "It proves that anybody— dogs, fish, whoever—can hold their breath for a long time."

"But Poo-Poo only held his breath for fifteen seconds," Stick Dog answered. "And while that is certainly a long time, it's not weeks and weeks."

Stripes said, "Close enough."

Poo-Poo and Karen nodded their heads.

"Yeah, Stick Dog," Mutt concurred. "It was close enough. What do you say we put this all behind us and go search for that fish tree?"

Stick Dog lowered his head and shuffled his front paws on the floor of his pipe. He smiled to himself. He loved how his friends all stuck together—even when they were totally wrong.

"Okay," he said upon raising his head. "Let's go look for that fish tree."

"Hooray!" Karen yelped as she, Mutt, Stripes, and Poo-Poo raced out of the pipe.

Stick Dog followed after them, but he did something else first. He picked up that paper sleeve that held those strange sticks. He read the words on it again.

Stick Dog knew they were not going to find a fish tree in the woods.

But he thought he knew something else too.

After reading the words on that paper sleeve, Stick Dog had an idea about where those sticks actually came from. He pulled the sticks out. He took that empty sleeve in his mouth and hustled after his friends.

Chapter 4

BURBLE-BURBLE-GLURP-GLURP!

As they ran through the woods, Poo-Poo, Stripes, Karen, and Mutt snapped their heads left and right, searching for the fish tree.

Stick Dog did not. He simply followed after them. He thought it might be best to let them *not* find the, umm, fish tree for a little while. But after several minutes of fruitless searching, Stick Dog was ready to change their approach.

"Hold on, everybody," Stick Dog called after dropping that paper sleeve from his mouth.

They were all tired and happy to take a break. Conveniently, there was a small grass-covered meadow where they stopped.

"What is it, Stick Dog?" panted Stripes. "Did you find the fish tree?"

"No. I didn't find the fish tree," he answered.

"Then what is it?" Poo-Poo asked with a tinge of impatience in his voice. "We're on a bit of a mission here."

"I just think there might be a better way to search for the source of those flavorful sticks," he said. "I was looking at this—"

"Wait a minute," Karen said. "I think I might know a better way myself."

"You do?" asked Stick Dog.

"I think so," Karen said, and began to pace back and forth in that small meadow. "Instead of running around all over the place looking for the fish tree, why don't we just stay right here and *call* to the fish tree and wait for it to answer. When we hear it, we'll just follow the sound!"

"Great idea," Poo-Poo said, and flopped down on

his belly. He seemed quite happy to have a little rest.

Stripes and Mutt thought it was a good idea too.

"We wait for the tree to answer?" Stick Dog asked.

"That's right," confirmed Karen.

"But trees don't, you know, talk."

"Of course the fish tree doesn't talk, Stick Dog," Karen said. She seemed a bit surprised at Stick Dog's lack of fish tree knowledge.

"Then how will it answer your call?"

"It's not the tree that answers, silly," Karen

said. "It's the fish *in* the tree that we'll hear."

Hello! Who is calling me?

"You mean the fish that grow in the tree and hold their breath for days and days to survive?"

"Exactly."

"Okay, then," Stick Dog said, and nodded. He figured it was probably easier just to stop questioning any of this. He wasn't frustrated. He had, after all, listened to plenty of his friends' bizarre theories and strategies over the years. "Why don't you go ahead and call the fish tree, Karen? And we'll see if it answers."

Karen nodded, pleased that Stick Dog was accepting of her plan. She took a deep inhale of air, preparing to yell out into the woods. She waited and held her breath.

And then let that great gush of air out.

"What's the matter, Karen?" asked Stripes.

Mutt asked, "Is something wrong?"

Poo-Poo yawned.

"I don't speak fish language," Karen explained. You could tell she was disappointed. "How am I supposed to call to the fish in the fish tree if I don't even speak their language?"

Stick Dog hung his head. He realized this might take longer than he originally thought. As he gazed down, he examined that paper that had held those flavorful sticks. The more he thought about it, the more he believed he might just know where those sticks came from.

And he was anxious to find out if he was right.

"Karen," he said, lifting his head. "You know, I think fish often blow bubbles when they're swimming around. I've seen bubbles rise and pop on the surface of the creek. And I'm pretty sure some of those bubbles come from fish. Maybe you should yell out some bubbly sounds. Maybe the fish in the, umm, fish tree would respond to that."

"Great idea, Stick Dog!" Karen exclaimed. She had gone from disappointed to excited in an instant. "I'll give it a try!"

She took another big breath of air—and then yelled out.

"Burble-Burble-Glurp!" she called. "Burble-Burble-Glurp-Glurp!"

BURBLE-BURBLE-GLURP!

She tilted her head to the left to listen for a response. Stripes, Mutt, and Poo-Poo listened intently as well.

"Did anybody hear the fish tree answer?" Karen whispered.

Nobody had.

Karen tried again.

"Burble-BURBLE!" she yelled even louder.
"Glurp-GLURP!"

Silence.

And more silence.

"The fish in the fish tree don't seem to be
listening," Karen announced to the group.
"What should we do, Stick Dog?"

"Well, first I want to tell you something
very important," he said to Karen.

"What's that?"

"I just want you to know that those bubble sounds were excellent," Stick Dog said. "I mean, I thought there were actual bubbles coming out of your mouth for a minute. It's a great skill that I didn't know you had."

"Wow, thanks," Karen responded proudly. "You know what else I'm good at?"

"What?"

"Chasing my tail!" she exclaimed. "Watch this!"

Then Karen chased her tail.

While she did that, Stick Dog picked up that slender paper sleeve and brought it closer to the group. He situated himself in the center

of his friends, dropped the paper, and
waited for Karen to finish.

When she was done chasing her tail after
a minute or so, Stick Dog said, "That was
fantastic, Karen."

"Thanks," she panted.

"Even though I'd like to continue our search
for the fish tree," Stick Dog said, "I think
maybe this paper package might help lead us
to those flavorful sticks. I think it has a clue
on it."

"It does?" Stripes asked. "Why did you wait
so long to tell us?"

Chapter 5

REVEALING THE CLUE

"Come look at this," Stick Dog said, and nodded down at the paper sleeve. He wanted them to get a good look at that package before it got much darker. Late afternoon had turned into early evening—and the daylight was beginning to fade. "I think there's a clue here."

Mutt, Poo-Poo, Karen, and Stripes examined the paper sleeve as Stick Dog read the words on it.

"'Lakeside Sushi Restaurant. Fish Is the

Dish!'" he read. "There's even a picture of a fish on it."

"So, what's the clue?" Stripes asked.

"'Lakeside Sushi Restaurant' is the clue," Stick Dog said. "I think the sticks came from this restaurant."

"What's sushi?" asked Poo-Poo. "I've never heard that word before."

"Me neither," Stick Dog answered honestly. "I think it must have something to do with fish. But we do know the word 'restaurant.' Humans eat lots of different foods at restaurants. And the word 'lakeside' is easy to figure out—I'm pretty sure it means by the side of a lake."

Mutt, Poo-Poo, Stripes, and Karen all looked at Stick Dog with puzzled expressions. Mutt seemed to talk for all of them when he asked, "I'm still not getting it. Where's this so-called clue you've been talking about, Stick Dog?"

"Umm," he said, and paused. He wanted to explain himself clearly and concisely. He wanted to keep his answer simple and short. "I think there's a fish restaurant near a lake."

"But there are millions of lakes all over the world," Stripes moaned. "How will we know which lake to look at?"

"That's true, Stripes," he answered. "But there's only one lake around *here*. Lake Washituba. It's past Picasso Park and through a small patch of woods."

"So what do you think we should do, Stick Dog?" asked Poo-Poo.

"I think we should, you know, go to that lake and see if there's a restaurant there," Stick Dog said. He thought that much would be obvious, but apparently it wasn't.

Mutt, Stripes, and Poo-Poo all thought this was a pretty good plan. But Karen wasn't quite so certain.

"I don't know about this," she said, pulling her mouth to one side and squinting her eyes a bit. "I still think calling out to the fish in the fish tree might be the way to go."

"Yes, that is a good plan too," Stick Dog said as seriously as he could muster. "I tell you what, Karen. As we go to the lake, how about if you keep calling out those bubbly sounds intermittently? And if the fish answer, we'll find that tree."

"What does 'intermittently' mean?" asked Karen.

"It means you'll call out to the fish tree every now and then," answered Stick Dog.

"Okay," Karen said, satisfied with this approach.

"All right," Stick Dog said, and smiled. He was happy to get their quest started. He turned in the direction of Lake Washituba. "Let's roll."

Mutt, Poo-Poo, and Stripes followed Stick Dog through the woods.

Karen did not.

She had something to do first.

She yelled, "Burble-Burble-Glurp!"

Chapter 6

INTERESTING MARRIAGES

Stick Dog led the way through the woods. He wove in, out, and around clumps of brambles, fallen tree branches, and honeysuckle bushes. It took several minutes to reach the edge of Picasso Park.

Stick Dog scanned the park from the forest line. He saw two big humans walking along the exercise path, but they were moving in the opposite direction. He didn't expect to see any little humans—and he didn't. With dusk approaching, he knew most of them were inside their homes getting ready for dinner.

"It's all clear," Stick Dog said to his friends as he stepped out of the woods.

Mutt, Stripes, Poo-Poo, and Karen emerged from the forest.

"Where's Lake Washituba?" asked Stripes.

"It's on the other side of the park, past the swing set and the basketball courts," Stick Dog said, and pointed. "And then through another patch of woods. We still have a ways to go. But the coast is clear. We should be able to get there pretty quickly."

"Did you say past the basketball courts?" asked Karen.

"That's right."

"The basketball courts where my favorite garbage can is?" Karen asked.

"Yes," Stick Dog answered slowly. He knew where this might be going.

"Do you think we could take a break from our long and perilous journey to Lake Washituba?" Karen asked. "And check my garbage can for tasty scraps?"

"Umm," Stick Dog said, and thought about it for a few seconds. He didn't really want to delay their trip to the lake. The sooner they found out if there was a restaurant there, the sooner they might get some of those flavorful sticks. But he couldn't deny Karen's wish. She had found plenty of things to eat in that garbage can. He hid his reluctance and said, "Sure we can. We'll give it a quick check and then keep moving."

"Yay!" Karen said. She spun around a couple of times to express her excitement. "Maybe we'll find some barbecue potato chips!"

"Maybe we will," Stick Dog said, and smiled. He was already feeling better about his decision after seeing her excitement.

"I love barbecue potato chips!"

"I know you do."

"If I could, I would totally *marry* a barbecue potato chip!"

This caught the attention of Stripes, Poo-Poo, and Mutt.

"You can marry food?" Stripes asked.

"I don't see why not," Karen answered simply.

"If I was going to marry a food," Poo-Poo said, "I would marry a hamburger. No doubt."

"I would marry a pizza," Mutt said. Just thinking about such a prospect made him drool a little bit.

Stripes declared her matrimonial choice next. She said, "I would marry a taco."

"What about you, Stick Dog?" Karen asked, hopping up and down. "What kind of food would you marry?"

"I'm not sure," he said. He was amused by his friends' conversation. It was always entertaining when they got going on an interesting subject. "I'd have to think about it. But can I ask you guys a question about this idea?"

"Sure, Stick Dog," Mutt said. "What is it?"

"What if you married all of these foods—a barbecue potato chip, hamburger, pizza, and taco?" he said. "And then you got super-hungry. Wouldn't it be really hard to be married to something so delicious when you were totally hungry? What would you do?"

"It wouldn't be hard at all," Karen said immediately. "I know exactly what I would do."

"And what's that?" Stick Dog asked.

"I'd eat my husband," Karen said. "Or my wife. Whichever it is. Chow time!"

HUSBAND

"You would?"

"Sure, no problem," Karen said, and brought

a pretend barbecue potato chip—spouse to her mouth and ate it. "Muncha, muncha!"

"What about you guys?" Stick Dog said to the others. "Would you eat your husbands and wives too?"

"Sure," said Mutt.

"Absolutely," said Stripes.

"There's no question about it," Poo-Poo answered, and then explained a little more. "Hunger is way more important than love, Stick Dog. Everybody knows that."

HUNGER > ♡

"Hmm, I guess I didn't know that," replied Stick Dog. He eyeballed the basketball courts and swing sets on the other side of Picasso Park. "Come on. Let's get over to Karen's favorite garbage can and see if there are any scraps."

They got to that garbage can quickly.

But when they got there, they didn't look for scraps.

Something had got there before them.

And it was still there.

Chapter 7

THE VAST INFINITY OF
THE COSMOS

Something stuck out of Karen's favorite garbage can—and it twitched.

It was a tail.

"It's a squirrel!" Poo-Poo growled and tensed up. His body shivered with rage. "I'd recognize that type of puffy tail anywhere. There's a nasty, chittering, foul-smelling, squirrel beast in there!"

Nobody saw Stick Dog shake his head slightly as the squirrel discovery took place. He knew this would distract Poo-Poo— and, unfortunately, delay their trip to Lake Washituba.

Poo-Poo growled deeply from his belly— an angry, dark, and guttural growl.

The squirrel heard him—and emerged from the garbage can. It poked its head out over the rim, staring right at Poo-Poo and making sounds.

Chitter-chitter.

It brought something to its mouth.

Crunch!

"What's it eating?"
Stripes asked.

"That's a . . . a . . . a . . . ,"
Karen whispered. "It's
a . . . a . . . barbecue potato chip!"

Stick Dog closed his eyes for three seconds.
This had quickly gone from bad, to kind
of bad, to really, really bad. Not only was
there something in the garbage can. It was
Poo-Poo's archenemy—a squirrel. And that
squirrel was also eating Karen's favorite
snack—a barbecue potato chip—right in
front of her. He knew this whole situation
would take some time.

"Why you little varmint!" Karen scream-whispered as she took three short but powerful dachshund strides toward the squirrel. "Who do you think you are? That's my favorite garbage can! That's my favorite snack! It's rightfully mine!"

"Let's make this quick, you puffy-tailed demon!" Poo-Poo muttered as he prowled two steps nearer. "It's time for the famous Mister Poo-Poo to do some serious squirrel damage!"

Karen and Poo-Poo were side by side, stepping closer to that garbage can—and closer to that squirrel.

"Don't worry, Karen," Poo-Poo whispered as they stalked. "I'll take care of this chittering devil. And you can get that barbecue potato chip."

"Deal," Karen whispered, and stopped. She held out her front right paw.

Poo-Poo paused too, looking Karen right in the eyes. He gave her a definitive paw-bump.

The squirrel noticed this brief moment when the two dogs were not watching— and leaped from the garbage can.

"There it goes!" yelped Stripes.

That squirrel was fast. Super-fast. It raced across the basketball court in four seconds, headed in the direction of the swing set. Poo-Poo and Karen jerked their heads to watch it, then pivoted and raced after it.

"You guys, wait!" Stick Dog called to try to stop them.

But it was no use.

Stick Dog hurried after them. Mutt and Stripes followed Stick Dog. It didn't take long for them to catch up.

Poo-Poo and Karen were at the bottom of the swing set staring up. And the squirrel was at the top of the swing set staring down.

"Ha!" Poo-Poo exclaimed when everybody was back together. "We've got that sniveling varmint totally trapped! Can you see?"

"I see, yes," Stick Dog said.

Karen asked, "What should we do now, Stick Dog?"

"I think," he answered, and thought of an idea quickly. He didn't know if it would work, but decided to give it a try. "I think you two have proven who is the best around here. Why, you've trapped your enemy in absolutely no time at all. I think you've already won this battle. Congratulations! Now we can go to Lake Washituba and look for that restaurant with the scrumptious sticks."

Karen and Poo-Poo turned to look at Stick Dog.

So did Mutt and Stripes.

Poo-Poo spoke for all of them when he said, "That's the most ridiculous thing I've ever heard."

"It is?" asked Stick Dog.

"Of course," Poo-Poo said. "After all my years in pursuit of squirrels, I finally have one trapped. And you want me to leave?!"

"I understand," Stick Dog said. He was disappointed, but he thought his idea was probably a long shot anyway. "Then, what *do* you want to do now?"

"I want to get up there, that's what!" Poo-Poo declared.

Stick Dog asked, "How are you going to do that?"

"I don't know," Poo-Poo admitted. He turned to Stripes, Karen, and Mutt. "Do you guys have any ideas?"

"Whatever we do, we better do it fast," Karen said quickly, and pointed at the squirrel. "It's almost done eating my barbecue potato chip!"

This realization brought an even greater sense of urgency to their problem.

"Okay," Poo-Poo said quickly. "How can I get up there?"

"Rocket ship!" Stripes suggested.

"Hot-air balloon!" Mutt yelped.

"Jet pack!" Karen yelled.

"Excellent!" Poo-Poo exclaimed. He was happy his friends had plenty of ideas. He turned toward Stick Dog and asked, "Do you have a rocket ship?"

"Me? A rocket ship?"

"Yes, you. A rocket ship."

"Umm, no," Stick Dog answered.

"That's okay, Stick Dog," Poo-Poo said. "I'm a little disappointed that you don't have a rocket ship. But don't worry about it. Don't let it get you down. I'm fine with it. I'm not mad or anything."

"That's good. I guess."

"Yeah, no rocket ship, no problem," Poo-Poo continued, "As long as you have a hot-air balloon, I'm good to go."

"Poo-Poo, I don't have a hot-air balloon either."

"Seriously?"

"Seriously."

"So, let me get this straight," Poo-Poo said. There was more than a hint of frustration in his voice. "You don't have a rocket ship *or* a hot-air balloon? Is that right?"

"That's right."

"Oh, wait!" Poo-Poo said, hope coming back to him as he remembered Karen's idea. "What about a jet pack?"

Stick Dog stopped responding to Poo-Poo's questions for a moment. He looked over the forest and toward the sky. It was dusk now and the moon was visible. He drew a few deep breaths as he took in the vastness of the sky and the light reflecting from the moon. He watched a single cloud as it passed slowly far above the treetops.

"Stick Dog?" Poo-Poo asked.

He gazed out past the moon.

Beyond the solar system.

Farther than the Milky Way galaxy.

And into the vast infinity of the cosmos.

"Stick Dog?" Poo-Poo asked again.

"Yes?" he whispered.

"What are you doing?"

Stick Dog didn't answer, but Karen answered on his behalf.

She said, "I think he's trying to remember where he put that jet pack."

"Stick Dog?" Poo-Poo repeated.

"Yes," he answered, lowering his head and smiling at his friend. He had regained a sense of calm. "What do you need?"

Poo-Poo said, "I was just wondering if you remember where you put that jet pack."

"I don't have a jet pack," Stick Dog said. He was happy he took a moment to himself. This back-and-forth conversation no longer made him anxious and antsy. He now found it funny. He still wanted to get to Lake Washituba as soon as possible, but he was determined to not let this delay bother him.

"You don't?"

"I don't," Stick Dog said. "But I think I know how to get up there."

Chapter 8

PUSHING AND SWINGING

"How do we get up there?" Poo-Poo asked Stick Dog.

"Well, since I do not have a rocket ship, hot-air balloon or jet pack at the moment," Stick Dog answered, "I've come up with a different plan."

Mutt, Stripes, Karen, and Poo-Poo gathered around Stick Dog in a semicircle. Poo-Poo shot a fierce stare at the squirrel every few seconds.

"What's your plan, Stick Dog?" asked Mutt.

"I think we should use the swings," he answered. "You guys get on the swings and I'll push you. You'll get higher and higher and maybe one of you will be able to reach the squirrel that way."

"I've never been on a swing before," Stripes said nervously. Mutt, Karen, and Poo-Poo all looked anxious as well.

"I know," Stick Dog said. "But we've seen plenty of little humans play on the swings. We know how they work. And the little humans always seem to be having a good time. I think it might be fun."

This nudge of encouragement was enough to convince Stick Dog's friends to give it a try.

It took a minute or two for them all to get situated in the swings. They realized that sitting back on their haunches was way more difficult than simply lying across the swing seats on their stomachs. It was much easier that way balance-wise.

The only hiccup was getting Karen up onto her swing. She was a little too short to get up by herself. But Stick Dog gave her a boost and she managed to get situated comfortably after that.

"Are you guys ready?" Stick Dog asked.

They said they
were.

And Stick Dog started to push. He went
down the line of swings pushing each of his
friends one time, then moving on to the
next. He pushed Poo-Poo first, then Karen,
Stripes, and Mutt. When he was done with
Mutt, he hustled back to Poo-Poo to start
the pattern over again.

You are probably wondering how this is
going to work out. Because, just like Stick
Dog, you know that those swings will never
get anywhere close to that squirrel. That's
because not only do swings go *up*, they also
go *out*. They never get near the bar at the
top where they hang from.

But Stick Dog knew that.

His plan was to end this whole thing and get to Lake Washituba as soon as possible. And his idea had absolutely nothing to do with reaching that squirrel.

I'll show you.

He pushed gently at first, making sure that his friends got used to the motion and could keep their balance. Mutt, Stripes, Karen, and Poo-Poo all commented as they swung.

"Whee!"

"Higher, Stick Dog, higher!"

"It makes my stomach feel funny!"

"I can't wait to reach that puffy-tailed menace!"

After his third series of pushes, Stick Dog put his plan into action.

"Sounds like you guys are having fun," Stick Dog said after pushing Mutt a third time. He hurried back to Poo-Poo to start again. "I've seen little humans close their eyes as they swing. You should try that. Remember to hold on."

They all closed their eyes.

And the squirrel noticed.

Stick Dog winked at the squirrel.

He smiled at it.

He nodded his head down and away from
the swing set.

And the squirrel
scurried down—
and away.

Chapter 9

POO-POO IS IN THE DICTIONARY

"Hey, Stick Dog!" Karen called as she swung on her swing with her eyes still closed.

"Yes?" he answered as he pushed Poo-Poo.

"You know what I was thinking about?"

"What's that?" Stick Dog asked, pushing Karen.

"You know how swinging makes our

stomachs feel funny and all that?" Karen asked.

"I've heard you describe it, yes," Stick Dog replied, and pushed Stripes.

"So, I was just thinking about my belly and the funny way it feels," Karen continued to explain. "Then I thought about my belly and how nice it feels when it's full. And then I asked myself, *What would I like to fill my belly with?* And I, of course, thought of barbecue potato chips!"

"I'm sure you did," said Stick Dog, taking a brief break after pushing Mutt.

"And when I thought of barbecue potato

chips," Karen continued, "I thought of that squirrel and I—"

She didn't finish her thought.

She was interrupted by Poo-Poo.

"Squirrel!" he screamed. His eyes flashed open with anger. His head jerked up and around, searching for his evil archenemy. He began to wriggle out of the swing to get off. "I forgot all about that twisted, rotten, puffy-tailed monster! Erggh! I can't stand those puffy tails!"

Stripes and Mutt opened their eyes too, alarmed by Poo-Poo's rage—and volume.

While all this occurred, Stick Dog steadied each swing. His friends pushed themselves off and gathered beneath the swing set. They stared up at the horizontal bar above them.

"We all had our eyes closed, Stick Dog," Poo-Poo said, and snarled. "Did you see where that nasty, puffy-tailed devil went?"

"Hmm," he responded. Obviously, Stick Dog did know where that squirrel went, but he didn't want to lie to his friends. "It's definitely not up there anymore, that's for sure."

HMM...

"I know exactly what happened," Poo-Poo whispered.

"What happened?" Mutt asked. "Where did it go?"

"Squirrels are evil in so many ways," Poo-Poo began to explain. "But they're also tricky, conniving, devious sneaks. They can hide better than any animal in the world."

"For real?" Karen asked.

"For real," confirmed Poo-Poo. "I mean, think about it. I'm probably the best squirrel hunter on the entire planet. My squirrel-hunting skills are unmatched, I tell you. If

you looked up 'squirrel-hunting expert' in the dictionary, there would be a picture of me!"

Mutt asked, "There would?"

"I'm pretty sure, yes," Poo-Poo replied, and went on. "So, if you consider how awesome I am at squirrel hunting, then squirrels must be the best hiders in the whole world."

"Why's that, Poo-Poo?" asked Stripes.

"Because I've never actually, you know, *caught* a squirrel," Poo-Poo answered. "That totally proves it. I mean, if *I* can't catch a squirrel, they must be really, really, really excellent hiders."

This made perfectly good sense to Stripes, Mutt, and Karen.

Stick Dog didn't quite agree with Poo-Poo's logic, but he didn't mention that. He was ready to move on.

"I think you're right, Poo-Poo," he said. "That sneaky devil is out of sight. It could be anywhere. Heck, it might've run off to Lake Washituba."

Poo-Poo squinted one eye and sneered. He turned in the direction of the lake and whispered, "Let's go look for it there."

"Hey, Stick Dog," Mutt said. "While Poo-Poo is looking for that squirrel, we could

continue to investigate those tasty sticks."

"That's a great idea," Stick Dog said, resisting the urge to slap a paw to his forehead. "I wish I would have thought of that. Let's go!"

And they went.

Chapter 10

LAKE WASHITUBA

Stick Dog and his friends ran across
Picasso Park and through another patch of
woods. They stopped when they reached
the edge of those woods and saw Lake
Washituba. The lake was surrounded by
trees and a few cabins.

And something else.

Something that Stick Dog was about to discover.

"It's beautiful here," Stripes said as they stared out across the lake. It was darker now and the moon was bright. The moonlight reflected on the water.

But there was more than moonlight reflecting off the surface of Lake Washituba.

There was another light—colorful and bright.

Stick Dog followed it with his eyes to the edge of the lake—and then to a building. There was a neon sign on top of that building:

It had more than words. There were two fish and something else.

"Look!" Stick Dog said, pointing at the restaurant. "There it is!"

Karen, Stripes, Mutt, and Poo-Poo all turned to look where Stick Dog pointed.

"There's what?" asked Stripes.

"The sushi restaurant," Stick Dog answered, and pointed toward the building again. "The one on that paper package for the sticks.

This must be the place where they came from."

"I don't know, Stick Dog," Stripes said doubtfully. "It seems like we're missing some real, hard evidence. I mean, this place could be anything."

"Yeah," Poo-Poo agreed. "Where's the proof?"

"Umm," Stick Dog replied slowly. "The *sign* is the proof. It says 'Sushi.' It's all there."

"Maybe the sign is a disguise of some sort," Stripes suggested. "Maybe it's something else pretending to be a sushi restaurant. Did you ever think of that?"

"Umm, no."

"Maybe it's an airport," Poo-Poo chimed in. This made his other friends come up with their own ideas.

Mutt said, "Or a skyscraper."

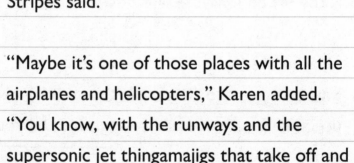

"Or a football stadium," Stripes said.

"Maybe it's one of those places with all the airplanes and helicopters," Karen added. "You know, with the runways and the supersonic jet thingamajigs that take off and land."

"You mean an airport?" Stick Dog asked.

"Yeah, yeah," Karen said, and smiled. She seemed happy that Stick Dog knew what she was talking about. "One of those."

Stick Dog inhaled deeply and turned his head to look out across the water. He watched as a breeze skimmed across the surface, creating hundreds of moonlit ripples. That wind made the water move just enough to create sound. He heard a canoe rock, slosh, and bump rhythmically against a dock near one of those cabins. He listened as the water brushed against the sand and rocks at the lake's edge.

Stick Dog listened as the water moved in and out.

SDLMM

He breathed in and out.

The water moved in and out.

He breathed in and out.

After that brief meditation, Stick Dog looked back at his friends.

"Of course, you might all be right," he said to his companions. "It most certainly *could* be an airport, a skyscraper or a football stadium."

"Or one of those places with the planes, like I mentioned," Karen said.

"Umm, right," Stick Dog said, and shook his head just a little. "I tell you what. I'm going to get a closer look. You guys find a good

place to hide around here and I'll be right
back."

They agreed to do this, and Stick Dog
stalked his way closer and closer toward the
restaurant.

At first, he stayed near the edge of the
forest. But about halfway there, he needed
to dart around a couple of the cabins near
the lake—and close to the docks in the
lake. Ultimately, he made it to a back corner
of the building, where he saw several cars
parked. He saw that a road ran along the
lake—and dead-ended at the restaurant.

Stick Dog moved to the side of the
building—and found an unusual window.

It had a small awning over it—and there was

a metal shelf outside of it. The area was lit by a large light attached to the brick wall. And there was a big female human standing right behind the window inside. She had a cloth wrapped around her forehead. And that cloth had a fish on it.

Hiding by a parked pickup truck, Stick Dog watched that window—and that human— trying to understand what it was all about.

It didn't take long.

That's because in less than a minute, a car

pulled up to that window. Stick Dog was in a perfect position to watch—and hear—what happened.

The human behind the window slid it open. She smiled at the human inside the car who had rolled his window down.

"Hello, Mr. Dalton," she said. "I thought I'd see you tonight. Thanks for calling your order in."

"Hi, Akira," the male human replied. "It's Tuesday. That's sushi night at our house."

"Everything's ready to go," she replied, and nodded. She turned, reached for a bag, and handed it out the window. "Maguro, inari, and tobiko sushi. And four maki rolls—two veggie, one salmon, one tuna."

"Perfect," the human in the car said, taking the bag. "Chopsticks?"

"In the bag."

"Awesome."

"'Chopsticks?'" Stick Dog whispered to himself. He wondered if this new word could refer to the tasty sticks that started tonight's quest. He didn't know why or how they were used, but he felt confident that could be their name.

After the two humans exchanged money and the car drove away, Stick Dog sought additional information. He stalked a slow, quiet arc to a front corner of the restaurant. Staying low, he peeked above the bottom edge of a window there.

Immediately, he could see why—and how—
the chopsticks were used.

"To pick up food?" Stick Dog asked himself
in a whisper. He'd never seen that before.
He had only seen humans pick up food
with their hands—or forks and spoons.
He watched, fascinated, as humans held
two chopsticks in one hand, pinched them
together, and picked up pieces of food from
their plates. Then they took that piece
of food, dipped it in a little dish of brown
liquid—and put it in their mouths.

"They use them to pick up food," Stick Dog
confirmed to himself. "Go figure."

Now that he had figured out the chopsticks,
Stick Dog focused more intently on the food
itself.

He saw brightly colored rolls cut up into equally sized pieces. He saw small slices of

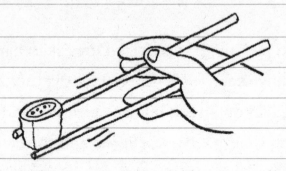

something—he suspected it was fish—on tiny beds of rice. Each human had a little dish of brown dipping sauce. He even found that green color they had tasted on those chopsticks back in his pipe. There were tiny clumps of green stuff that the humans sometimes stirred into their dipping sauces.

Stick Dog ducked down and away from the window.

He had gathered so much information.

He knew what sushi was.

He knew what chopsticks were.

He knew humans were eating sushi inside the restaurant—but he also knew humans came and picked up their sushi at that strange window.

Stick Dog moved more quickly now. He stayed hidden in the darkness, but he hurried back to share all this information with Mutt, Poo-Poo, Karen, and Stripes. He was starting to think that maybe—just maybe—they might get their paws on some of that sushi tonight.

He sprinted the last several yards to where he had left his friends.

He knew they were hiding. So, he called quietly to them.

"You guys?" he said. "I'm back."

"We're over here," Stripes answered.

Stick Dog turned his head toward where Stripes had called from—toward the lake.

He didn't see them right away.

"Stick Dog?" Poo-Poo called.

"Yes?" he answered, squinting his eyes and

trying to pinpoint exactly where his friends were in the darkness.

"Umm," Poo-Poo said. "We have a bit of a situation here."

Finally, Stick Dog saw where they were.

They *did* have a bit of situation.

A bad situation.

Chapter 11

MUTT DIDN'T HAVE A CHOICE

Stick Dog saw where his friends were.

They were in that canoe that he had heard bumping against the dock earlier.

But the canoe was no longer tied to that dock. It was adrift—floating very slowly farther and farther out into the lake.

"Oh no," Stick Dog whispered. He didn't want his friends to hear him—and panic. He hurried to the dock—and ran to its end. The canoe was out of reach, but close enough for him to talk with his friends. "What happened?"

"We did what you said," Stripes answered. "We got into this boat thing. We thought it would be a good place to hide."

"It is a good place," Stick Dog said. "But how did the canoe get detached from the dock? Why are you, you know, floating away?"

"Oh, that," Poo-Poo said, and pointed toward Mutt, who was situated near the back of the canoe. "Mister-I-Have-to-Chew-on-Everything-I-Find found the rope that tied the boat to the dock. He chewed through it in, like, twenty seconds."

Mutt heard this, looked up at Stick Dog, and shrugged, some rope hanging from his mouth. Stick Dog looked down and saw the other end of the rope tied to the dock.

"Is that true, Mutt?"

"It's true," Mutt mumbled before spitting that rope from his mouth and answering more politely. "I'm a dog. There was a rope. I chewed on it. What choice did I have?"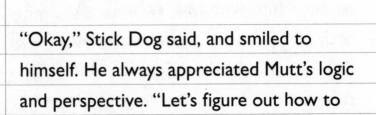

"Okay," Stick Dog said, and smiled to himself. He always appreciated Mutt's logic and perspective. "Let's figure out how to get you back here."

"No need to figure anything out, Stick Dog," Poo-Poo declared from the front of the canoe. "We've already come up with a plan."

"You have?"

"You betcha," Karen confirmed.

"We put all our minds together and came up with a strategy," Stripes said proudly.

"That's a lot of brainpower," Stick Dog said, and cleared his throat. He wasn't certain that he wanted to hear their rescue strategy. But they didn't seem to be drifting anymore—and he was pretty sure he knew how to get them back anyway. "What's your plan?"

"We just wait until tomorrow," Poo-Poo said.

Stripes said, "Until the sun comes up."

Karen added, "And it gets really hot."

Mutt didn't say anything. He was chewing that rope again.

"Okay, umm," Stick Dog said, and paused a few seconds. "How does that get you out of the canoe and back here to the dock?"

"When the sun comes out and the day gets hot," Poo-Poo explained, "the lake will evaporate. When all the water's gone, we'll just step out of this boat and walk to shore. Easy stuff."

"You want to wait until the lake evaporates?" Stick Dog asked.

"That's right," Stripes answered for the group.

Mutt chewed on the rope.

"Umm, I'm not sure—"

"We know it won't happen right away," Poo-Poo interrupted.

"We're willing to wait," Karen added. "We realize it may take a while. You know, ten—maybe fifteen—minutes."

Stick Dog asked, "You think it will take ten or fifteen minutes for this lake to evaporate?"

"At the most," Poo-Poo said. "Could be less."

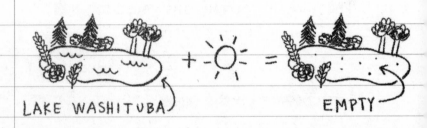

LAKE WASHITUBA + ☀ = EMPTY

"Okay," Stick Dog said. "What are you going to do until tomorrow? Until this big lake evaporates?"

"Two things," answered Stripes. "We've got that all planned out as well."

"Good for you," Stick Dog said. He looked around to ensure there were no humans coming. There weren't. He also confirmed that his friends weren't drifting too far away as they talked. They weren't. "What two things?"

"The first thing is sleep," Poo-Poo replied. "Get some rest. You know, this has been a pretty busy day and night."

"Good idea," Stick Dog said. "And what's the second thing?"

"We're going to eat some sushi!" Karen exclaimed. She was excited by that prospect. "Can't wait!"

"We've decided that you may be right," Stripes said, and pointed at the sushi restaurant. "We don't think that place is an airport, football stadium, or skyscraper any longer."

Karen added, "Or one of those places with all the helicopters and airplanes and runways and stuff."

"Good to hear," Stick Dog said. "How are you going to get the sushi?"

"That's the easy part," Poo-Poo said. "You just go get it."

"And bring it to us!" Karen shouted.

"I do?"

"You do," Stripes confirmed, and yawned. "Just wake us up when you get back with the sushi feast."

"Umm, okay," Stick Dog said slowly. "How do I get the sushi out to you in the boat?"

"You can just toss it," Poo-Poo answered. "We'll catch it."

"Great plan," Stick Dog said with more confidence. It seemed like something had occurred to him right then. It was as if he thought of a way to get his friends back to shore—and now he could make it happen. "Can we go over it one more time though? Just to make sure I understand?"

"Of course," Karen said.

Mutt chewed on the rope.

"First, you guys stay in the canoe," Stick Dog began. "Then you fall asleep. While you're all resting, I figure out a way to get some sushi from that restaurant that isn't an airport, skyscraper or football stadium—or, umm, the place with all the airplanes, helicopters, and runways. After I get the sushi, I come back here. I wake you up and toss you the sushi. You eat it and go back to sleep. We wait for daylight, the lake evaporates in ten or fifteen minutes—at the most. Then you step out of the canoe and walk to shore. Is that it? Did I cover everything?"

"Sounds like you did, Stick Dog," Stripes said, and yawned even bigger and longer than before. "Good work. Let us know when you're back with that sushi."

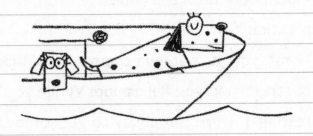

"Will do," Stick Dog said, but he didn't leave. "There's just one thing I want to make sure of before I go."

"What's that?" asked Poo-Poo.

"I need to make certain that I can throw something out to you guys," he replied. "It would be a shame if I came back with some sushi and then I couldn't get it to you."

"You're right," Karen agreed. "That would totally stink."

"For sure," Stick Dog said. "So I thought I would do a test throw or two. You know, practice a bit. Just to make sure."

"Sounds reasonable," Stripes said.

"Mutt," Stick Dog called. "I wonder if you could do me a favor?"

Mutt spit the rope from his mouth and said, "Sure thing. How may I assist you?"

"I need to practice my throwing," Stick Dog said. "Could you toss me the end of that rope? I think I'll practice with that. How long is it?"

"It's super-long," Mutt answered after dropping his head to look at the rope. "The other end is tied to a little metal loop in here. It's all coiled up and stuff. Why, I could chew on this rope for three or four years before swallowing and slowly digesting the whole thing."

"Great," Stick Dog answered. "Can you

throw the end to me?"

And that's what Mutt did. He took the rope's end in his mouth and made his way to the front of the canoe. When he got there, he twisted his head back and then jerked it forward, releasing the rope as he did.

It was a great throw. Stick Dog caught it on the first try.

He did not throw the rope back.

And he didn't practice. Stick Dog took the end of that rope and began to pull on it.

Mutt was right—it was super-long. He tugged on it for more than twenty seconds and the canoe didn't move.

"What are you doing, Stick Dog?" Karen asked. "I thought you were going to use that rope to practice throwing."

"I was," he answered as he continued to pull on that slack rope. The rope he had already pulled was gathered in a messy pile at his paws. "But then I thought I could just pull you in. That way we don't have to, umm, wait for the lake to evaporate tomorrow."

"What about the other part of the plan?" Poo-Poo asked. "When you bring us the sushi feast and all that?"

"Well, I was thinking," Stick Dog responded. The rope became tight as he talked. The slack was gone and his friends were now coming slowly closer. "I'm not sure I can get that sushi all by myself. I think I'll need your help."

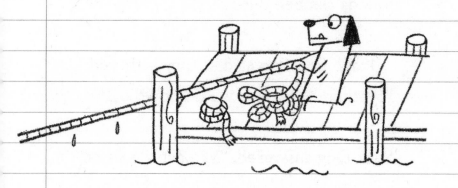

"That's certainly true," Stripes admitted. "I mean, if we had to count on you for everything, that probably wouldn't work out so great."

"Exactly," Stick Dog said. The canoe was almost to the dock. "I don't know how I'd get anything done without you guys. I mean, we're a team."

He pulled the canoe the rest of the way to the dock. He looped some of that rope around a metal hook on the dock as his friends climbed out.

"Okay," Poo-Poo said as they gathered together. "What do we do now?"

Stick Dog answered, "We get the sushi."

Chapter 12

POKING AND TICKLING

Stick Dog led his friends to where he had observed everything before. He pointed out that strange window. He described how humans would drive up to it and pick up their sushi. Then he led them to the front corner of the restaurant and they peeked inside.

"See the sticks we found in Mutt's fur?" Stick Dog asked. "I'm pretty sure they're called 'chopsticks.' The humans use them to pick up their sushi food."

Mutt, Karen, Stripes, and Poo-Poo all saw
what Stick Dog was talking about. And
they all remembered the flavors from those
chopsticks.

Poo-Poo's stomach rumbled. And right after
that, Mutt's, Karen's, and Stripes's stomachs
rumbled too.

Mutt turned to Stick Dog, wiped some
drool from the corner of his mouth, and
asked, "How are we going to get that
sushi?!"

"I don't know yet," Stick Dog admitted.
"But let's get away from this window. It's

way too dangerous here. We could get
spotted. We need to find a safe place to
figure it out."

They ended up near three metal garbage
cans in a dark spot where the road came
into the parking lot. The cans stood in some
grass at the side of the road. They settled
there to come up with a sushi-snatching
strategy.

They examined the garbage cans briefly,
hoping there might be some food inside.
They tapped each can and listened to the
hollow metallic sound it made. "I don't think
there's anything
in them," Stick
Dog said. "Let's
concentrate on
getting that sushi."

"I think we can use those chopsticks to get the sushi," Poo-Poo said. Apparently, he already had an idea. He spoke as he did a couple of circles, patting down the grass and leaves beneath him so he could lie down comfortably.

"How can we use them?" asked Karen.

Stick Dog only half listened to Poo-Poo. While he did, he thought about what he'd seen inside the restaurant and at that window.

"We use them as weapons," Poo-Poo answered.

Mutt asked, "Weapons?"

"Weapons," Poo-Poo confirmed, and

plopped down on his belly. "We wait for some humans to open the door of the restaurant to go inside. Then we sneak in behind them. Once we're inside, we grab as many chopsticks as possible and run around poking those humans as hard as we can. As they scream and squirm in agony, we just grab as much sushi as possible and hightail it out of there!"

CHOPSTICK WEAPONS

"Sounds great," Stripes said.

Karen and Mutt agreed.

But Stick Dog did not.

"I don't think we should, umm, poke the humans with the chopsticks—and try to hurt them," Stick Dog said.

"Why not?" asked Poo-Poo. He seemed a little offended that Stick Dog was not buying into his plan. "What's wrong with a little poking action?"

"Well, umm," Stick Dog said, and paused. It was like his mind was working on two problems at the same time. He needed to come up with some valid and reasonable reason to stop Poo-Poo's plan. And he also had to come up with a plan—one that might actually work—of his own.

"Yeah," Karen said. "Why not?"

"There are dozens of chopsticks in that

sushi restaurant," Stick Dog answered. "What if the humans all see us running around poking them with chopstick weapons? And then *they* pick up chopsticks themselves—and start using them as weapons against *us*? I don't want to get poked with a chopstick. Do you guys?"

"It's a fair point," Poo-Poo said, and cringed, thinking about that prospect.

Stick Dog was happy to have knocked that nutty idea down—but he still didn't have a legitimate plan of his own.

"Poo-Poo, maybe we don't have to abandon your plan entirely," Mutt suggested. "Maybe we should use those chopsticks in a different way."

"How so?" Poo-Poo asked. He seemed encouraged that his idea wouldn't be wasted.

"Instead of *poking* the humans with the chopsticks," Mutt explained, "we *tickle* the humans with the chopsticks instead. While they're all laughing and giggling, we snatch the sushi."

"Awesome!" Poo-Poo exclaimed.

Stripes and Karen thought it was a terrific idea too.

"Stick Dog," Mutt said, and nodded toward the restaurant. "We're going into the sushi place now to tickle the humans with the chopsticks. Are you coming?"

"Wait," he answered. "I don't think we should do that."

Karen asked, "Why not?"

"It's just that—" Stick Dog said, and hesitated. For the first time in a while, he couldn't think of anything to say.

But he didn't have to.

That's because right then two humans came out of that sushi restaurant—and headed straight at Stick Dog and his friends.

Chapter 13

TWO PUFFY-TAILED RASCALS

There was one big male human—and one big female.

They each carried two bulky garbage bags—
and one long, rubbery strap with hooks.

"Shh!" Stick Dog whispered urgently. He
pointed at the humans. "They're coming this
way! They're coming to the garbage cans!"

Mutt, Karen, Stripes, and Poo-Poo all stared
at the garbage-toting humans.

"What do we do?" Poo-Poo whispered.

"It's okay," Stick Dog answered as calmly
as he could. They had a little time, but not
much. The humans were all the way across
the parking lot. And they were not moving
fast—it looked like those garbage bags were
heavy and slowing them down. "There are
woods all around us. Just follow me. Stay
low and quiet."

Stick Dog crouched down, turned toward the woods, and got ready to sneak away.

But he didn't.

Stripes stopped him.

She said, "I'm not sure we should do what you say anymore, Stick Dog."

Stick Dog turned his head over his shoulder to look at Stripes. She didn't look mean or upset. It looked more like she was just stating a fact. He asked, "Why not?"

"Well, the last time you gave us instructions didn't turn out very well," Stripes explained. "Remember when you told us to hide while you checked out that airport or skyscraper or football stadium?"

"It's a sushi restaurant."

"We didn't know that at the time," Stripes said, and sighed. "But the point is, the last instruction you gave us was to hide."

"Was there something wrong with that?" Stick Dog asked in a whisper. Those big humans were a third of the way to them now.

"Don't you remember how it turned out?" Stripes answered, whispering too. Stick Dog was thankful that she had followed his lead and talked quietly. "We ended up floating out into the lake! See what happens when we follow your instructions? I mean, at the very least, I think you should take some responsibility for the dangerous predicament you put us in. Don't you think?"

For a single second, Stick Dog considered taking a little time to himself. Maybe he could cast his eyes somewhere again and focus on calm, steady breathing. But their time was slipping away. The humans were closer. He even worried that sushi restaurant could close soon.

"You know what, Stripes?" he said. "I take

full responsibility. I don't know what I was thinking."

Thankfully, this was enough for Stripes.

They did as Stick Dog instructed. Crouching down to their bellies, Mutt, Poo-Poo, Karen, and Stripes scurried away from those three metal garbage cans as quietly as they could. Stick Dog led them into the woods at the side of the road. They didn't need to go very deep to be well hidden.

Stick Dog didn't want to go too far. He wanted to watch and listen to the humans. He hoped that maybe—just maybe—they would do or say something that might help him.

The two humans reached the garbage cans.

"This is such a pain in the neck," the female said as they both dropped the garbage bags next to the metal cans.

"Definitely," the male answered. He went to one can and the female went to another. "All because of those puffy-tailed rascals."

"Hopefully, these new straps will work," the female said. "And keep those troublemaking varmints out."

"They must be talking about squirrels!" Poo-Poo whispered excitedly from behind an oak tree trunk. "I *like* these humans!"

"Shh," said Stick Dog.

The humans took the lids off.

"It better keep them out," the male said as he put his two bags into one can. The female put her bags into another can. "Those raccoons got into these cans again last night. It took half an hour to clean up all the trash. It was all over the road."

They put the lids on and stretched the straps across the top. They hooked the straps on to the handles of the garbage cans. Then they walked back to the sushi restaurant.

"It isn't squirrels they don't like," Poo-Poo said. He sounded sad. "It's raccoons."

"What's wrong with that, Poo-Poo?" asked Mutt.

"Nothing really," he answered. "It's just I feel a special bond with anybody else who doesn't like squirrels, that's all."

"Well, think about it this way," said Stick Dog. He wanted to make Poo-Poo feel better. "Those humans don't like *puffy-tailed* raccoons. And you don't like *puffy-tailed* squirrels. So, you do have a special bond—a

unique dislike—for puffy-tailed creatures."

"Hmm," Poo-Poo said, and thought about this for a moment. Then his tail wagged. "Yeah."

With Poo-Poo feeling better and the humans gone, Stick Dog relaxed a little— and got back to thinking.

"The sushi is only three places," Stick Dog said to himself. "Inside the restaurant. At the strange window. Or in a car after someone drives away."

"What are we going to do, Stick Dog?" Stripes asked. "Should we get in the restaurant? You know, go back to that chopstick-tickling plan that was mentioned earlier?"

"Let's use that as an emergency backup plan," Stick Dog said quietly. "We might be able to get into that restaurant, but getting back out would be tough—and dangerous, I think."

"What about doing something at the window?" asked Karen.

"I just don't see how that could work either," he said, and shook his head a bit. "The human inside the window hands the bag of sushi to the human driving the car. I mean, there's always a human hand grasping the bag."

Poo-Poo suggested, "We could jump up and bite their hands. I bet they'd let go of the bags then!"

"Umm, maybe," Stick Dog said. "I don't think

it's a good idea to go around biting humans though. But we can call that emergency backup plan number two."

"Okay," Poo-Poo said, and nodded. He seemed satisfied enough with that.

"What about jumping into the car when it drives away?" asked Mutt. "We could try that."

"No way. Moving cars are always—always—dangerous," Stick Dog replied. He placed a paw on his chin. His brow was furrowed. He looked frustrated.

And his friends saw—and sensed—his frustration.

"Ugh," Poo-Poo said. "Maybe we should give up. Maybe we should just stop."

"Yeah, Stick Dog," Stripes said, and sighed. "I'm tired. Let's stop."

Karen added, "Stopping might be best."

Mutt shook a sky-blue mitten from his fur and began to chew on it.

It was, Stick Dog knew, a very rare occurrence for them to be this close to the end of their food quest—and not succeed. He also knew it was even more rare for his friends to give up like this.

And he knew something else too.

He knew how they might get that sushi.

Chapter 14

SMARTASTIC

"I've got it," Stick Dog said. "And you guys helped me figure it out just now."

"How?" asked Karen.

"By using the word 'stop' over and over."

"I'm not surprised," Stripes chimed in. "I mean, it's usually the four of us who solve our problems, Stick Dog."

He didn't respond to this particular comment, but Stick Dog did nod his head a bit and smile.

"So, how do we get the sushi?" Mutt asked, tucking that sky-blue mitten back into his fur to chew on later.

"Like I said, there are only three places to get that sushi," Stick Dog said as his friends gathered around him. "*Inside* the restaurant. *At* the window. Or *in* the car."

Mutt, Poo-Poo, Karen, and Stripes were no longer frustrated and defeated. Now they were nervous and excited. They couldn't wait to hear Stick Dog's idea—and they couldn't wait to get that sushi. Karen hopped up and down.

"We're not going into the restaurant,"
Stick Dog continued. "And we're not doing
anything at the window."

Stick Dog moved around the group with his
eyes, staring briefly at each of his friends
with strength and conviction.

He said, "We're going to use the car."

"But you said moving cars are always—
always—dangerous," reminded Poo-Poo.

"You're right, I did," Stick Dog said. "But
what if the car isn't moving? What if we
stopped it?"

"How in the world can we do that?" asked
Stripes.

Before he could answer, Poo-Poo had an idea.

"We could use a bulldozer!" he yelped.

This made the others come up with plans too. Stripes, Mutt, and Karen shouted out their own ideas in succession.

"We could use a toothbrush!"

"Or a flamingo feather!"

"Or one of those places where the planes and helicopters and runways are!"

Stick Dog decided instantly not to ask his friends about how they would use a bulldozer, toothbrush, flamingo feather, or airport to stop a moving car. Stick Dog just told them his idea.

He said, "We're going to create a blockade to make a car stop."

His friends looked at Stick Dog with puzzled expressions. Karen asked the question that was on all of their minds.

"What's a blockade?"

"Oh, sorry," Stick Dog said. "It's a new word. A blockade is—"

But he didn't get the chance to answer.

"I got this, Stick Dog," Poo-Poo interrupted. "I know lots of words. Dozens even. When it comes to words, I'm quite smartastic."

"Smartastic?" Stick Dog asked.

"Yeah. It means really, really smart. It's a word you don't know, but I do. See what I mean?"

"Okay, Poo-Poo. I, umm, see what you mean," Stick Dog said. He sat back on his haunches. He had the distinct feeling this might take a minute or two. "What's a *blockade*?"

"It's when two humans are acting all lovey-dovey," Poo-Poo said, obviously a little uncomfortable with the subject. "And one human gets down on one knee and sings a song up to the other human, who is leaning out a window. The song is real romantical. And then the human in the window has a bunch of hearts fly out of their chest."

There was silence then. Utter silence. For eight seconds. Then Stripes spoke.

She whispered, "Humans are so weird."

"I have a question about this romantical blockade," Karen said, and started to giggle. "Does it have to be humans? Could it be—oh, I don't know—Stick Dog singing to Lucy perhaps? How about it, Stick Dog? Have you ever sung lovey-dovey blockades to Lucy?"

"I think you might be thinking of a *serenade*, Poo-Poo," Stick Dog said, and then worked to avoid Karen's question. "And I think Poo-Poo's right. Serenades are only for humans. So, I don't see how that could answer your question, Karen, since I'm a dog."

"I know what a blockade is, Stick Dog."

"Okay, Mutt," Stick Dog said. He was very happy to move on. "Tell us. What is a blockade?"

"It's a creature that's made up of two different things—the top of a female human and a long tail-thing of a fish," Mutt answered. "Heck, there might even be one of those blockades right here in Lake Washituba."

"That's a *mermaid*," Stick Dog said kindly. "But you're right. There might, umm, be one here in the lake."

"So, I was mostly right?"

"Sure," answered Stick Dog. "Mostly."

Mutt seemed pleased by that.

"I'm smartastic too," Stripes said, stepping forward. "So you won't be surprised to learn that I know the definition of blockade."

"That wouldn't surprise me at all," Stick Dog said, and leaned back against a tree stump. This was taking longer than he thought it would. "What is it?"

"It's when a bunch of humans go down the street," Stripes said confidently. "And there are marching bands and big balloons and clowns and decorated cars and stuff."

"You might be thinking of a *parade*," Stick Dog said.

"Same difference," Stripes said. Then she rubbed her belly against the ground to scratch it.

It was Karen's turn. She obviously didn't want to be left out.

"I'm *super*-smartastic," she said. "And I can, without question, tell you exactly what a blockade is."

"Let's hear it."

"A blockade is a small bug-and-worm type thing," Karen said. "It moves forward by scooting on all its little legs and arching its back. It likes to eat leaves. And it's fuzzy. They're actually pretty darn cute!"

"Karen," Stick Dog said, and coughed a bit. "What you're describing is a caterpillar."

"I am? That's what you call those things?!" Karen asked. "I never knew their names! And when I heard this new 'blockade' word, I just thought I could use it for them. Caterpillar, hunh? How about that? Caterpillar,

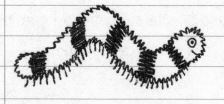caterpillar, caterpillar! They sure are cute! Aren't they, Stick Dog?!"

"They sure are," Stick Dog said, and laughed. He loved how overjoyed Karen was. He got back up to all fours, made certain no more humans were about, and said, "Now, can I tell you what a blockade is?"

They all said he could.

"A blockade is when you create an obstacle in the path of something to stop it," Stick Dog said. He realized that his friends might not know the word "obstacle" either, so he simplified his definition. "You make a blockade to stop something from moving."

Poo-Poo asked, "What do you make a blockade with?"

"You can make one with just about anything," Stick Dog answered. Then he pointed at the three metal garbage cans. "We're going to use those."

Then he pointed down the road where it curved by the lake. They could all see the headlights of an approaching car in the distance.

"And if that car is coming to pick up some

sushi from that window," Stick Dog said with fierce determination, "then that's the car we're going to stop."

They all stared at the car as it got closer.

And closer.

And closer.

Chapter 15

LET'S ROLL

Stick Dog believed there was an excellent chance that the approaching car was coming to the sushi restaurant. There were only a few cabins between them and the car. He thought it was likely the human inside was a sushi customer.

"Okay," he said, speaking quickly. "This car could be going three places. It could be going to one of the cabins. It might be parking in the lot and the humans inside will go into the restaurant. Or it will pull up to the window."

"Why would it pull up to the window, Stick Dog?" Stripes asked.

"To get the sushi."

"Oh, right."

"If it goes to the window, we go make the blockade," Stick Dog explained, and eyeballed that car as it grew nearer. "We'll have to hurry. It doesn't take much time for the human inside the car to pick up and pay for their sushi."

The car passed the final cabin. It was definitely coming to the sushi restaurant.

"If the car pulls up to the window," Stick Dog said, "we run to the garbage cans and use them to make a blockade across the road."

"How do we do that?" Poo-Poo asked.

"I'll get the rubber straps off the two cans with garbage inside," Stick Dog said quickly, turning his head away from the glare of that car's headlights. The dogs were well hidden, but those headlights were quite bright in the dark night. "Then we'll push them over, pull out the garbage bags, and spread everything across the road to create the blockade. We want to do everything as quietly as possible."

"How do we get the sushi?" Mutt asked. "After the car stops?"

"The human driver will have to get out of the car to move the garbage cans and trash," Stick Dog answered. "When the human gets out, I'll try to get into the car and grab the sushi."

He looked at his friends as the car passed slowly by on the road.

Their faces were serious. Their bodies were tense. Their stomachs rumbled.

They were ready.

And so was Stick Dog.

He watched the car as it reached the parking
lot.

It didn't park.

It went straight to the window.

Stick Dog said one thing.

One simple thing.

"Let's roll."

Chapter 16

BUSTED

Mutt, Stripes, Poo-Poo, and Karen followed Stick Dog as he raced away from that hiding spot at the edge of the woods. They got to the metal garbage cans in fourteen seconds.

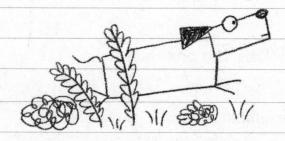

"I'll get these straps off," Stick Dog whispered when they got there. It was dark where the road emptied into the parking lot. He was pretty confident they could not be seen from the restaurant. "Then we'll pull the bags out."

"Okay, Stick Dog," Mutt answered for the group.

"Remember, we have to be quiet," Stick Dog added. "We don't want anyone coming out here before the blockade is built."

He found out quickly that the metal hook at the end of the strap was too smooth to grasp with his paws. But by biting on it he could get a grip. He pulled on the hook—down and then out—and got it off the handle. He could feel the strap go slack as the tension released. He pushed the loose strap through the handle on top of the lid. He decided to push it over after working on

the second strap on the other can. It would
be quiet longer that way.

Now that Stick Dog knew how to do it, he
thought the second one would be easy—
and fast.

And it needed to be fast.

That's because he took two seconds to
jerk his head and look toward that car and
strange window. It was open and the female
human inside was talking and smiling with
the human—another female—in the car.

And she was handing her two bags of sushi.

"She still has to pay and drive over here," Stick Dog whispered to himself, and turned his attention to the second garbage can with a rubber strap.

He bit down on the hook, began to pull it— and stopped.

He didn't stop because he hurt his teeth. Or because the rubber strap pinched him. Or because a human was coming. He stopped because he heard a sound.

Wham! Crash! Boota-boota-boota.

Stick Dog yanked his head to find the source. It only took two seconds for him to figure it out.

BOOTA-BOOTA-BOOTA

Here's what he saw.

The empty garbage can was on its side and rocking a little back and forth. It had just rolled to a stop. The can's lid was clanking and wobbling on the road too. Karen, Stripes, and Mutt all stared right back at Stick Dog.

And Poo-Poo's eyes were squeezed shut as he rubbed his head.

"Poo-Poo?!" Stick Dog scream-whispered. "Did you bash into that garbage can headfirst?"

"Hunh?" he answered, still
rubbing his head.

"The can? Did you just bash into
it with your head?"

"Of course I did," he answered.
"I'm Poo-Poo."

"It was SO loud!" Stick Dog said, doing his
best to not let his frustration show.

"It was?" asked Poo-Poo.

"Didn't you hear it?" asked Stick Dog.

"Not really," Poo-Poo answered. He had
stopped rubbing his head and opened his
eyes. "You know, whenever I bash my head
into something, there's kind of a dull buzzing

in my brain. I don't hear anything at all for several seconds. Maybe that's why I didn't hear it."

"Maybe so," Stick Dog replied, not knowing what else to say.

Stick Dog turned quickly toward the restaurant again. Something was happening at that window that he didn't expect. The big female human leaned out the window, squinted her eyes—and stared right at Stick Dog.

She looked angry.

I KNOW YOU'RE OUT THERE!

"I know you're out there!" she yelled.

Stick Dog held stone-still.

They were busted.

He had no idea what she could do next. She could come running out here with other humans. She could call a dogcatcher.

"We're going to have to run for it," Stick Dog whispered to his friends. Mutt, Karen, Poo-Poo, and Stripes were all frozen in place too. "We're not going to get the sushi. We need to try another time."

His friends didn't complain. They knew Stick Dog was right.

"Okay," Stick Dog said, remaining still and whispering. He thought about the best—and safest—route back to his pipe under Highway 16. He knew humans were probably coming, but he also knew they had a minute or so before any human could get there from the restaurant across the parking lot. "We'll go straight into the woods right now. Then we'll make a long arc around the sushi restaurant. It's dark, so we'll have to go slow, but we'll be far away from any humans. Follow me."

 Stick Dog took his first step toward the woods—and stopped.

That big female human yelled in their direction again.

She yelled something Stick Dog didn't expect—not at all.

Chapter 17

HA-HA! GUESS WHAT?

The big female human was still leaning out
that window and staring toward Stick Dog
and his friends.

"Get out of there,
you gosh-darn
raccoons!" she
yelled. "I can't see
you, but I can hear
you! I know you're
out there! Scram!
Get! Go!"

"She thinks we're raccoons?!" Karen said quietly. "She doesn't know the difference between a dog and a raccoon? What a wack-a-doodle!"

Mutt, Poo-Poo, and Stripes all giggled a little bit.

"She thinks we're raccoons," Stick Dog whispered to himself. How could that be? She was staring right at them. He could see her clearly in the bright light around the window. He twitched. He understood. "We can see her, but *she* can't see *us*. She just *heard* us."

He waved in her direction.

No reaction.

"Ha-ha! Guess what?" the human yelled. "You lousy raccoons can't get the lids off now!"

Stick Dog sat back and waved both his front legs at her.

No reaction. The female inside the restaurant turned her attention back to the customer in the car.

"Sorry about the yelling," she said. "It will be just a minute for the rest of your order. I'll be right back."

He turned to his friends as the female human inside the restaurant slid the window shut and disappeared—and the female human in the car rolled her window up.

"She couldn't see us because she was in the light—and we're in the dark," Stick Dog explained quickly. "She just thinks there are raccoons out here because she heard Poo-Poo knock over the garbage can. I don't think she's coming out or calling a dogcatcher."

"Stick Dog?" asked Stripes.

"Yes?"

"How do you think I would look with a raccoon tail?"

"Umm, what?" Stick Dog asked. Considering their current circumstances, he definitely wasn't expecting this kind of question.

"Well, I was just wondering," Stripes went on. "You know, she thinks we're raccoons and everything. I just think it would be interesting if my whole body was covered with my magnificent spots—*and* I had a striped tail. It would be quite a unique combination, don't you think?"

"I think so, yes."

"And I'm quite unique myself, aren't I?"

"You are certainly unique," Stick Dog said, and smiled.

Stripes liked that. She wagged her tail and strutted around a bit.

"I think we can still build the blockade and stop that car!" Stick Dog said quietly, turning serious—and urgent—again. "It might work!"

That's all Poo-Poo, Mutt, Karen, and Stripes needed to hear. They worked with Stick Dog, pushing the other two garbage cans over. They pulled two garbage bags out and spread them across the road.

Stick Dog didn't care about being quiet anymore. After all, they had already been discovered—sort of. The humans had heard them—though they thought the dogs were raccoons. Plus, the restaurant and

car windows were closed now. Without the
need to be quiet, they got their blockade
built quickly.

The dogs pushed and dragged and yanked
the metal garbage cans and lids into position.
It all scraped and clanked and rang against
the blacktop.

They were done with their blockade in
thirty seconds.

They took several seconds to admire their
work.

"For being brand-new at this blockade
business," Poo-Poo said, "I'd say we're pretty
darn good at it!"

After all that frantic work and noise, the

night turned suddenly silent as they looked at the blockade. You could hear a breeze through the trees and water splashing softly at Lake Washituba's shore.

Then there was another sound.

The car's engine revved a little bit.

Stick Dog turned to look at it. He realized instantly that the customer must have gotten the rest of her order.

"The car's coming!" he said. "Follow me!"

They reached the woods in eleven seconds. They ducked behind some weeds, bushes, and brush and stared at that car as it slowly approached. Its white headlights got bigger and brighter as it rolled closer.

And closer.

And stopped.

"It worked!" Stripes exclaimed in a whisper. "Our blockade totally worked!"

Stick Dog smiled slightly, but he knew their mission wasn't complete yet. He figured it would take that big female human only a minute or so to move those garbage cans out of the way so she could continue home.

"You guys stay here," he said, and ducked down as low as he could.

"I'm going to try to get into the car."

Stick Dog reached the edge of the road and heard the engine turn off.

The big female human opened the driver's-side door—and got out.

"Please leave the door open," Stick Dog whispered.

"Oh, for goodness' sake," the female human said as she got out of the car. "That girl was right. Those raccoons really are a nuisance. What a pain."

"*Please* leave the door open."

She did.

Stick Dog watched as she walked in front of the car and began to put the garbage bags back into the cans, stand the cans upright, and drag them back to the side of the road.

"This is going to be easier than I thought," Stick Dog whispered. It was going to take her at least a minute—maybe more—to move all that stuff out of the way. The car even acted as a perfect shield. Stick Dog was confident he wouldn't be seen as he grabbed the sushi.

He stalked around the back of the car, staying low and stepping quietly. He climbed onto the front seat and saw two bags of sushi on the passenger seat.

He smiled—and reached for the bags.

And stopped.

There was someone else in the car.

Chapter 18

'MERE!

As Stick Dog reached for the bags, he heard
two sounds come from the backseat.

He heard a gurgle—and a giggle.

He turned his head
slowly—very, very
slowly—to find out
what made those
sounds.

A small female human was in a strange seat
back there. She had two bows in her hair.

Her legs kicked wildly—not in a mean way, but in an energetic, excited, fun way. She

giggled some more and reached both of her hands out toward Stick Dog, squeezing her pudgy, little fingers open and shut.

"C'mere!" the little human squealed, and giggled again. "'Mere!"

Stick Dog was stuck. He was afraid if he grabbed those sushi bags and hustled away, he might startle—maybe even scare—her. She might yell or cry—and that would get the big human's attention immediately. But he also knew he had to hurry. He could hear the big human dragging the second garbage can to the side of the road.

"'Mere!"

He had to satisfy this little human—*and* get out of there as fast as he could.

"'Mere!"

He leaned slowly toward the little female human. He tilted his head a little.

She petted the top of his head—and scratched him behind the ear.

Stick Dog closed his eyes and leaned closer—it felt good.

But he had to go. He could hear the big human outside the car as she dragged the third and final garbage can to the side of the road. Stick Dog pulled his head back slowly to the front seat. The small human gave him three pats on top of the head as he did.

Those felt good too.

"Ba-ba, woggy!" she said after the third pat.

Stick Dog was pretty sure it was okay to leave now.

He grasped the two sushi bags with his mouth and backed slowly out of the car.

"Ba-ba, woggy!"

Crouching down low, he headed back to his friends. He made certain to keep that car between himself and the big human female so he wouldn't be seen. Stick Dog could hear the big human as he headed back to his friends.

"Well, that's done," she said, and clapped her hands after the third garbage can was off the road. "Rotten raccoons."

He heard her walk back to the car.

Stick Dog stopped and turned to look at the car. He was safely hidden in the dark behind a tall patch of weeds. He watched the big human get in the car, reach back to the small

human, and tickle her beneath the chin.

"What were you laughing about in here, you silly goose?" she asked. "Who were you talking to?"

Stick Dog couldn't tell if that small human answered or not.

The big female human closed the door, started the car, and drove away.

He wondered when she would notice the sushi was missing.

Just to be safe, Stick Dog waited until that car's red taillights were far away. Then he returned to his friends.

Chapter 19

STICK DOG GETS SOME ADVICE

Karen asked, "What do you have there, Stick Dog?"

He put the bags down on the ground and answered.

"The sushi," he said, trying really hard not to shake his head and sigh. "Remember? We built that blockade? And the car stopped?

And I snuck into the car and grabbed the bags?"

"What a great plan that was," Karen said with admiration in her voice. "Who thought of that?"

"It was, umm, all of us," Stick Dog said. "It was a team effort."

Karen said, "Good for us."

She, Poo-Poo, Mutt, and Stripes came close to the bags and sniffed them.

And drooled.

PUDDLE
OF
DROOL

"Come on," Stick Dog said. "Let's find a place with a little light so we can see what we're eating. Mutt, can you carry one of these bags for me?"

"I'd be happy to, Stick Dog."

They ended up back at the dock where the canoe was. With the moon and the distant light from the restaurant, they could see the sushi.

After figuring out how to get the plastic lids off the aluminum containers, they spread all that sushi out on the dock. There were five rolls cut into six pieces each. There were slices of fish on little beds of rice. They discovered those little mounds of green pasty stuff smelled spicy. And there were thinly sliced pink things that smelled sweet.

"It's time for the chopsticks," Stripes said hurriedly. You could tell she wanted to eat as soon as possible. She and Mutt ripped open some of the paper sleeves and passed out chopsticks to everyone as quickly as they could.

"You guys want to use chopsticks?" Stick Dog asked. He was honestly surprised at this.

"Of course," Poo-Poo said. "That's the way you eat sushi. We saw the humans doing it in the restaurant."

"Yeah, Stick Dog," Karen said. "How else would we do it?"

"You're right, you're right," he replied. He didn't want to delay getting to that sushi any longer. He didn't believe his friends would want to use those chopsticks for very long—not with all that sushi just waiting for them.

He watched as they tried to pick up the sushi with chopsticks.

None of them could do it. It was hard to hold the sticks with their paws. It was even harder to pinch the chopsticks together to pick up a piece of sushi.

Mutt almost got a piece by stabbing a chopstick through one of the pieces, but it slid off when he brought it to his mouth.

"Errrrggh," Poo-Poo moaned after failing on

his fifth attempt. "This is impossible!"

The others were just as frustrated.

"What should we do, Stick Dog?" Stripes asked.

He was expecting this.

"Well, I think the way to eat sushi for *humans* is with chopsticks," Stick Dog said calmly. "But I think the way to eat sushi for *dogs* is different."

"How do dogs do it?" asked Karen with hope—and hunger—in her voice.

"I think we lean down and get a piece with our mouths," answered Stick Dog. "And, you know, eat it."

They all smiled at him—and dropped their chopsticks to the wooden dock.

The sushi was delicious.

They shared all the different kinds. They saved the sweet pink things for dessert.

They were finished eating in less than five minutes.

With full bellies, they were instantly sleepy.

Stick Dog saw his friends' eyelids get droopy. Poo-Poo was already lying down— and almost asleep. Karen and Stripes walked toward Mutt, thinking they would settle in next to him.

"It's getting late," Stick Dog said before everybody got too comfortable. He knew they couldn't sleep here. "We have to get back to my pipe."

"We could just get in this boat and sleep there," Stripes suggested, nodding toward the canoe. "Nothing bad could happen in there."

"Yeah," Mutt agreed. "I wouldn't mind chewing on that rope some more."

Stick Dog didn't mention that the last time they were in the canoe, Mutt chewed on the rope—and they drifted out into the lake.

"No, I don't think we should do that," he said.

"Why not?"

"Well, last time it was the four of you," Stick Dog said. "With me it would be five of us. It might be too much weight—especially after eating all that sushi. It might sink."

None of them liked that idea.

"You're probably right," Karen said, and looked at Stick Dog—sort of examining him. "It does look like you've put on a couple of pounds."

"Maybe you should start working out, Stick Dog," Poo-Poo said as he pushed himself up to all fours and stretched.

"You should take better care of yourself," Mutt said as they walked off the dock. "You're not getting any younger, Stick Dog."

They followed Stick Dog to the woods. At the forest's edge, he stopped and let his friends go first.

"Thanks for the advice," he said. He pulled a branch aside so his friends could enter easily. He was happy to be on the way home.

"Let's face it, Stick Dog," Stripes said, turning left to follow Poo-Poo, Mutt, and Karen. "You'd be lost without us."

"Um, guys," Stick Dog said, and smiled. He pointed to the right. "It's this way."

THE END.

P.S.

Some people say it's okay to give dogs sushi, some say it's not. Now, Stick Dog and his pals (especially Mutt) will eat anything. They're stray dogs, they're hungry all the time. They have to eat whatever they can find. They've developed super-strong stomachs for that reason. So they did fine with sushi. But it might be best not to offer your dog sushi. Try a hamburger instead. Or a hot dog. Or pizza. Or donuts. Or spaghetti. Or barbecue ribs. Or mashed potatoes. Or tacos. —TW

Tom Watson lives in Chicago with his wife, daughter, and son. He also has a dog, as you could probably guess. The dog is a Labrador-Newfoundland mix. Tom says he looks like a Labrador with a bad perm. He wanted to name the dog "Put Your Shirt On" (please don't ask why), but he was outvoted by his family. The dog's name is Shadow. Early in his career Tom worked in politics, including a stint as the chief speechwriter for the governor of Ohio. This experience helped him develop the unique storytelling narrative style of the Stick Dog, Stick Cat, and Trouble at Table 5 books. Tom's time in politics also made him realize a very important thing: kids are way smarter than adults. And it's a lot more fun and rewarding to write stories for them than to write speeches for grown-ups.